This book belongs to

... ...

Also by Matt Beighton

Poetry

Tig You're It: And other poems from the playground

The Shadowland Chronicles

The Spyglass and the Cherry Tree

The Shadowed Eye

Monstacademy Series

The Halloween Parade

The Egyptian Treasure

The Grand High Monster

The Machu Picchu Mystery

The Magic Knight

For Younger Readers

Spot The Dot

For all the little monsters

MONSTACADEMY
THE GRAND HIGH MONSTER

Printed in the United Kingdom
First Printing, 2019

A CIP catalogue record for this book is available from the British Library.

ISBN (Standard Edition): 978-1-9161360-2-1
ISBN (Dyslexia Friendly): 978-1-9161360-3-8

www.mattbeighton.co.uk
www.monstacademy.com

MONSTACADEMY

The Grand High Monster

MEAN

GHOULS

CHAPTER 1

A Sticky Situation

"Ummmf—" Trixie Grimble was cut off mid-scream as a thick green slime rose out of her beaker and swallowed her head.

It was the first day back at school after a long summer holiday, and her first day as a second year at Monstacademy. Her first year hadn't gone as well as she hoped, and she'd been forced to be a hero on more than one occasion. Not only that, she'd managed to make a devoted enemy of, and seriously annoy, more than one teacher. All this before she'd even turned eleven.

In fact, one teacher was currently in prison because of Trixie and her friends Gloria (a vegetarian vampire) and Colin (a cursed werewolf who turned into a poodle at full-moon). And now here she was, not even making it to lunchtime before being attacked by her science experiment.

"Trixie!" Gloria called out from across the wooden bench. In a panic, she ran around and tried to scrape the goo from her friend's face, but it was too thick. She shouted for help from the teacher,

a wizened old vampire called Mr
Snickletinkle. The vampire waddled
over and threw a beaker of warm,
yellow liquid over Trixie's head.
The ooze started to melt away, and
soon Trixie was able to gasp for
breath and eventually calm down
enough to talk.

"Thank you so much, sir! I don't
know what happened. It was
supposed to be a potion to cure
baldness!" she stammered.

"That's quite all right, Miss
Grimble. These things happen."

Ever since she'd joined
Monstacademy as the only non-
monster, Trixie had been fighting
a reputation as a clumsy buffoon.
Luckily, some of the teachers were

more understanding than others.

"What did you throw over her?" Gloria asked.

"It was a mixture of rosewater, herbs, mysterious salts and a large dose of *Ranae Defricatus Urina*!"

"Rana what now?" Trixie knew better than to trust anybody who gave a Latin name for an ingredient. It was often a way of hiding what it really was.

Gloria, who paid more attention in Miss Brimstone's Latin classes and who, unlike Trixie who had annoyed Miss Brimstone so consistently, wasn't forced to face the wall during lessons, spluttered, "Frog...wee?"

"Indeed, Miss Toothsome. It dissolves most slime quite effectively."

Trixie clawed at her face and tried desperately to wash it with cold water from the tap. Heston Gobswaddle, who was older than Trixie and her friends but who had been held back repeatedly for refusing to listen in lessons, had wandered over during the whole debacle and was doubled over with laughter.

Heston and Trixie didn't get on at all, and he loved nothing more than a chance to laugh at her misfortune. It annoyed Trixie just how often those opportunities came about. This year she had vowed to be much less clumsy but, so far, it wasn't working.

"At least it's over," she muttered to Gloria. "Heston will get bored soon and move on."

Gloria was staring past Trixie's shoulder and looked very worried. "I wouldn't be so sure of that!"

When Trixie turned, her heart sank. The potion had continued to grow and had swallowed the glass beaker. It had flowed out and onto the wooden bench and was making a swift break for the floor. It was frothing up as it moved, a bit like the bubbles in your washing up bowl at home. Soon, Trixie and Gloria could barely see the rest of the equipment on their desk, and the potion was almost ankle-deep on the floor.

Mr Snickletinkle had finally noticed the chaos and was trying his hardest to get the other children to calm down and form a line at the door. Because children can never be trusted to do as they are told, especially when green slime is heading their way, they were running around and screaming instead.

"Stay away from the bogeys!" some were screaming.

"The floor is made of snot!" shouted a smart-aleck at the back of the room.

Some of the braver ones were

daring each other to try and jump over the slime or splash through it like a paddling pool. Those that tried soon found out just how sticky it was. Cries of *"My shoe!"* and *"It's got my foot!"* and *"Tell my mother I love her!"* echoed around the classroom but were barely heard above the screams. Mr Snickletinkle was running around the classroom moaning about how he'd never find enough frogs to clear the mess up.

Before long, the runaway slime had reached the door, and each and every child was stuck firmly in place. Most were simply glued by their feet to the floor. Some of the sillier children had decided to sit down and were now stuck to chairs by the seat of their pants. Cyril Clump, a tiresome little know-it-all, had tried to scramble up the wall and was now stuck hanging by one hand a metre above the floor.

By now the noise was deafening which turned out to be very lucky as Miss Brimstone, the wailing banshee who also happened to be the deputy-headmistress and who had been investigating why there was a frothy mess heading towards her office, heard the shouts and slowly made her way through the door. She was careful to only step on the small sections of floor that hadn't been covered in slime. She ended up walking like a constipated flamingo, much to the enjoyment of the children.

"What is the meaning of all of this?" she screeched through a crack in the door.

"I'm terribly sorry, Miss Brimstone. One of the students had a small accident with their baldness cure, and, well, you can see the result. I believe they added bottled badger burp by mistake." Trixie blushed. Even Mr Snickletinkle sounded timid in the face of Miss Brimstone's wrath.

"This student, it wouldn't happen to be Trixie Grimble by any chance, would it?"

Trixie's face went an even deeper shade of red. "Sorry, Miss Brimstone. I didn't mean it."

"You are in a lot of trouble, Miss Grimble. Do you have any idea how difficult and expensive this will be to clean up? And at such an important time. You really have outdone yourself this time. And to add insult to slimy injury, the poor school cat is out here stuck to the floor. The rat that it was chasing is stuck right next to him! It's sticking its tongue out and taunting the poor thing!"

In the end, it took over an hour for all of the slime to lose its stickiness enough for everyone to escape and run off for a long, hot shower. Trixie didn't stick around to see how long the actual clean up would take. She didn't have a chance to clean up herself before she was grabbed by a still angry Miss Brimstone and escorted to the office of the vampire headmistress, Miss Flopsbottom.

On the way, Trixie noticed a very smug-looking school cat with a long pink tail hanging out of its mouth. She smiled at the thought of Heston's rude little rat meeting such a sticky end.

Miss Flopsbottom showed Trixie into her office and offered her a seat in front of her large wooden desk. When she sat down behind it, Trixie realised just how sad the large headmistress looked. It was like looking at a crying puppy, and Trixie found herself wanting to do anything to cheer her up again.

"I am so disappointed in you," the headmistress started. It didn't help Trixie's mood. "It is the first day back...we haven't even had lunch yet...I just don't know what to do." Miss Flopsbottom couldn't seem to settle on what was upsetting her the most. "Trixie, what do you have to say for yourself?"

Trixie stayed quiet. What was there to say? She really didn't mean to do these things. She had no idea why they kept happening to her. Didn't Miss Flopsbottom realise that she would stop in a heartbeat if she could?

"I don't suppose you know this, but we are being visited by the Grand High Monster in a few weeks. He is the head of all Monsterdom in Europe. He controls the schools and businesses that we Monsters rely on to live our lives. If he comes here and it doesn't all go swimmingly...it just doesn't bear thinking about."

Miss Flopsbottom rubbed her eyes. Trixie could see that they were red with tiredness. The headmistress stressed about most things, but Trixie had never seen her like this. She worried about what it might mean. She didn't have to worry for long. "This is one accident too many, Trixie. You leave me no choice. I have to suspend you from Monstacademy."

CHAPTER 2

Verity Dogsby

In the end, Trixie was only suspended for a week, but it felt like the longest week in the world. When it was over, she couldn't wait to return to Monstacademy. Her time at home had been spent at the bottom of the garden in the leaking shed.

Trixie's mother had moaned and whined about how it was such an important time in the training schedule for Grimble's

Cat Cacophony, so Trixie had just wandered off and tried her hardest to avoid her mother altogether.

Now she was back at school she was eager to get back up to speed with what she had missed, and so she had made her way down to the main hall for breakfast. She found Colin in their usual corner and sat down against the cold stone wall next to him.

"Where's Gloria?" she asked. Colin pointed to a table on the other side of the hall. Gloria was sat down next to what appeared to be a sack of rocks. "Who's that?" she asked.

"I don't know her name. She's new, though. Started while you were gone. Apparently, she's a transfer from Cromley's. She's a troll I think. Never had one of those here before. The cook had to go to the quarry to get her some food!"

"What's Gloria doing with her? Does she know her from somewhere else?"

"I don't think so. She's just starting sitting with her in lessons, and now they eat together as well. They asked me to sit with them but, well, you know how it is with the other werewolves."

Trixie nodded but inside she was upset. It wasn't just the troll. Gloria was sat with other vampires and werewolves: all of the popular kids. Trixie and Colin had nicknamed them the Mean Ghouls at the end of the last term. She frowned when she saw that Esme Furfang was hanging out with them as well. Trixie wasn't surprised but, after reaching a sort of happy truce at the end of the last term, she'd hoped they might be able to get along this year.

As they watched, one of the girls pulled out a small pink book, and they all started giggling at whatever was inside it. Trixie had seen it before; they carried it everywhere with them. Colin reckoned it was filled with secrets and horrible rumours about everyone in the school. She thought it was more likely to be stuffed with secret potions to make everyone else's clothes out of fashion. They weren't nice monsters.

Why did Gloria need a new friend? Surely the three of them were enough.

"It's been boring without you here, I know that much," Colin said when she pointed this out.

Muttering under her breath, Trixie decided to take action. She wandered across the hall and sat down next to Gloria. At first, her friend didn't notice her, so she coughed politely. Gloria spun in her seat and gave Trixie a huge hug.

"This is Verity. Verity Dogsby,"

she introduced the troll to Trixie.

"Isn't she so different and exciting!" squealed one of the annoyingly pretty werewolves. "Isn't it great that she wants to be our friend?" Trixie recognised her as Angua something-or-other. Gloria started to introduce her and the other Mean Ghouls, but Trixie cut her off quickly.

"Nice to meet you." Trixie wasn't really interested in Gloria's new friends. Instead, she wanted to know why her best friend had left Colin on his own.

"Oh, he's okay!" Gloria laughed. "I asked him to come and sit with us. He really needs to grow up and get to know the other werewolves, you know. They aren't that bad. Verity has been introducing me to them. Some of them are a bit bawdy, but I think Colin is being a bit too sensitive."

Trixie couldn't believe what Gloria was saying. She refused to sit with the other vampires because they drank blood, and here she was expecting Colin to become friends with the werewolves who constantly teased him about being a werepoodle.

"Well, I'm going to go and sit with my friend," said Trixie angrily. She stood up and walked back over to Colin. Behind her, she heard the two girls giggling amongst themselves.

"I really don't know what has gotten into her," she said to Colin when she had sat back down next to him. "She's not acting like herself at all."

"I don't like that troll."

"Her name's Verity Dogsby."

"Whatever. I don't like her at all. Why has she moved here from Cromley's?"

"Why does it matter that she's come from Cromley's? I thought we got on well with them," Trixie asked. They had shared a Halloween Parade the year before, and Trixie had been very impressed with their floats, not to mention the fact that their banner said exactly what it was meant to.

"We were."

"Why aren't we now? What happened?"

Colin leaned in as though he was about to whisper a dark and dangerous secret. "It's all about the money, you see. My dad works for the government, the Monster government," he added as he saw Trixie's eyes widen. "He said that there's not enough money to keep two monster schools open in the area anymore, and so one of us has to close."

"That's awful!" cried Trixie, a little more loudly than she meant to. Colin clapped his hand over her

mouth to keep her quiet.

"It is, but Monstacademy is a lot bigger than Cromley's, and we do better in exams. Really it will probably be Cromley's that closes. That's why she's here. She's moving before the school closes, I bet."

"Well, how will they decide which school closes?" Despite Colin's positivity, Trixie was very worried. She didn't want to lose Monstacademy now. Ironically, she didn't want to go back to an ordinary school now. Plus, she'd lose all of her new friends. Even worse, she might end up being home-schooled by her mother – though she suspected it would end

up being a crash-course in circus-cat training, more than anything else.

"I don't know, probably politics or something." He shrugged his shoulders.

"Miss Flopsbottom told me that we are having a visit from the Grand High Monster soon. Could that be anything to do with it?"

"Yeah, probably." Colin didn't seem too worried at all. "He's a big cheese, that's for sure. If he likes Monstacademy, we'll definitely stay open, I reckon." Colin looked up from his breakfast and pointed to where their friend had recently been sat. "Hey, where's Gloria gone?"

Trixie shrugged. It wasn't like her to leave the hall before breakfast was finished. Only final-year students were allowed to leave before being told to do so, and Gloria never liked being in trouble.

"They didn't walk past us. Trust me, the Mean Ghouls can't walk past anybody without saying something snarky. The only other way out is the door to the teacher's tower. Why would they be going up there?" Now it was Colin's turn to shrug. "We should go find out."

Colin looked glum. Trixie knew how much he hated snooping around and going on adventures.

She got the feeling he only ever went along with it to keep her and Gloria happy. Nevertheless, he finished his bowl of cereal (Shredded Woof) and dragged himself to his feet.

"Come on, then!" He led Trixie to the back of the hall, making sure that none of the teachers spotted where they were heading. When they reached the door, they darted through and closed it quietly behind them. Trixie's heart was beating hard in her chest.

She'd done a lot of things wrong by accident during her time at Monstacademy, but this was the first time she'd done it on purpose. Sneaking into Heston Gobswaddle's

dormitory didn't count. He'd been up to no good, and everybody knows that you can break the rules if you are stopping a no-good deed.

They'd planned on heading to the top floors of the tower where Miss Flopsbottom's and Miss Brimstone's offices were, but on the second floor, they heard whispered voices coming from behind an old wooden door. The sign on the front read:

GRIMSBY'S - KEEP OUT!

Grimsby, a small, patchwork man covered in more stitches than a quilt, was the school caretaker and often spent the days outside in the gardens mowing the lawns or chopping trees down or playing fetch with his pet parrot. Most of the older children seemed to have taken it upon themselves to lay silly traps for him around the school, and now he tried to keep himself to himself as often as possible.

The voices coming from his office were definitely not his, there was no lisp. Trixie recognised Gloria's voice straight away, and the other sounded like somebody walking along a gravel driveway. Definitely the voice of a troll. She pulled Colin to one side, and they both pressed their ears to the door.

Before they managed to hear anything, the door swung open and Trixie very nearly stumbled into the room. Instead, she swung out an arm to steady herself and hit Verity straight across her stone chin. Trixie was sure that it hurt her hand a good deal more than it hurt Verity, but she still started to apologise profusely.

"Hang on," Colin interrupted her apology. "Before we start apologising, I want to know what you two were doing in Grimsby's office. Does he know you were there?"

"It's nothing. We got lost!" Verity's gravelly voice was deep and rough and not at all believable.

"Where are the rest of the Mean Ghouls?" Trixie said it before she could stop herself.

"Oh, grow up!" Verity scoffed. "They roll with me now, and I've made them all honorary trolls. We're actually thinking of calling ourselves the Rocks."

"I was just helping out my new friend," Gloria said nastily, changing the subject quickly.

"It really doesn't matter anyway. We need to get going." Verity seemed uncomfortable and tried to kick Gloria in the leg. Unfortunately, a kick in the leg from a troll is hard to ignore, however subtle, and Gloria started hopping around shouting.

"What did you do that for? I was

just going to tell them that I was helping you to find the plans for the layout of the school." Gloria turned to Trixie and Colin, who looked bemused. "She wanted to know how such an amazing building was built, that's all. She's very interested in architecture!"

If it was possible for somebody whose face was made of stone to look sheepish, Verity managed it.

It was lost on Colin though who had had enough. "Let's leave these two friends alone, Trixie. None of us is supposed to be here anyway, and I'm not getting into trouble for her." He stuck his tongue out at Gloria and dragged Trixie away with him and back down into the main hall.

They spent the rest of the day trying to avoid bumping into their former friend.

CHAPTER 3

The Grand High Monster

The Grand High Monster was, as Colin said, a big cheese in the Monster world. He or she was a bit like the Prime Minister for Monsters. The current Grand High Monster was a man by the name of Reginald Trompington the Third. When he walked into the main hall of Monstacademy at lunchtime on the following Monday, you could have heard a pin drop.

He was a giant of a man, ten

feet tall and as broad as a bus. His face was covered in a thick black beard that hung past his waist, and his eyebrows looked like two hairy caterpillars lining up to fight each other at the top of his nose. He wore a thick leather hat on his head with a peacock feather stuck in the brim. To protect against the

summer rain, he was wearing a long, bottle-green overcoat.

When he spoke, his voice rumbled and echoed around the silent hall like an elephant burping in church. Behind him were stood a dozen smaller men and women dressed in sensible black suits and rather boring bowler hats. They looked a bit like bodyguards but ones who would be more likely to write you a stern letter than actually tell you off.

"Where can I find a—" Reginald Trompington the Third looked down at a sodden piece of paper that looked lost in his enormous hands, "Mrs Floppy Bottom?"

Trixie glanced across the hall and

caught the Mean Ghouls giggling to themselves. Gloria had started wearing her hair in a bun wrapped in a grey scarf like the others. Apparently, it made their hair look more troll-ish.

"Er, that's Miss Flopsbottom, Your Monsterness!" squeaked Miss Flopsbottom as she stood up quickly at the teachers' table. She moved so quickly towards the Grand High Monster that her sensible heels kicked up sparks on the flagstones.

"Exactly, that's what I said!" he roared. "I suppose you are in charge of this place?"

"Yes, sir. Me and my excellent teachers, of course!"

Trixie had never seen the headmistress in such a fluster. If she flapped her arms any more, she'd take off and fly out of the window!

"Right! Well, I'm here to see the excellent work that you are doing. Informally, of course! Wouldn't want you to think that there was anything formal or important about this at all!"

"Yeah, right!" whispered Colin. "Nothing important at all!" He winked at Trixie knowingly.

"Would you care to join us for lunch?" asked Miss Flopsbottom. She was busily shooing the other teachers along the bench to make room for Mr Trompington's giant bottom. Mr Snickletinkle fell off the end and landed on the floor with a pathetic squeak.

The Grand High Monster and his guards all took a seat at the teachers' table (most of the teachers had to move, some even gave up altogether and left the dining hall) and started to tuck into the piles of food.

"This doesn't look good." Colin didn't seem as confident as he had before, Trixie noticed. "Those people with him are the Auditors. They look at everything in the school and see if it's good enough or not. If anything goes wrong or if anything isn't quite right, they can close you down. Scary people!"

Trixie was worried. If anything was going to go wrong, she had a horrible feeling that it would be her fault. Maybe Miss Flopsbottom had hoped that the Grand High Monster would turn up while she was suspended. She knew that she had to be on her best behaviour for as long as the Auditors were at Monstacademy.

"How long do they stay for?" Trixie asked Colin later that day as they sat doing their homework under a large apple tree. The rain had made way for a lovely sunny evening, and Trixie was still trying to avoid Gloria and Verity who had taken to doing their homework in the dormitory.

"It depends really." Colin didn't look up from his Latin homework. Trixie could see over his shoulder that he'd got most of the answers wrong but didn't have the heart to tell him. "Sometimes they only stay for a week, but my dad told me that at Schweineunten in Germany they were there for nearly a year! It was awful.

"He said that several of the teachers disappeared and were never seen again. Some of the children, too! He reckons that the headmaster got worried and put a spell on them and forgot how to get them back. Bad times!"

Trixie couldn't help but think that Colin was a little bit too excited about the idea of teachers disappearing. "I hope Miss Flopsbottom doesn't get any ideas. I'll be gone quicker than you can say whistling wombats!"

Colin didn't laugh at Trixie's joke. Instead, he looked grumpily over her shoulder. Trixie swivelled her head to see Gloria, Verity and the rest of their gang laughing and giggling their way across the courtyard towards the apple tree.

"Just ignore them," she whispered. "I can't be bothered to have an argument with her at the minute."

They didn't have to go to the effort. Gloria turned her head away as soon as she saw Trixie and

Colin and headed in the opposite direction.

"I just don't get it." Colin looked glummer than Trixie had ever seen him. "She was fine until you went away, and then suddenly, Verity joins the school and Gloria is off gallivanting with her and the other Mean Ghouls. I blame Miss Brimstone."

"Why's that?" asked Trixie.

"She asked Gloria to help Verity settle in and get to know everyone. The next day, Verity was showing Gloria some pieces of paper, and suddenly she's staring at me across the classroom like I've puked in her breakfast. It's really weird. I don't trust that Verity at all."

"Me neither," said Trixie with feeling. "But don't worry, we'll get Gloria back. I'll have a word with her in science this afternoon and see what's going on."

"Thanks. Whatever it is, I just want to know so I can say sorry. Or at least give her a clever insult!"

In the distance, the bell announced the beginning of the afternoon's lessons, and the two of them stood up wearily and made their way back to the tall tower that held their science classroom.

CHAPTER 4

A Plane Mistake

By the time Trixie and Colin burst
into Mr Snickletinkle's lesson, the
diminutive, elderly vampire was
already halfway through explaining
whatever potion was the focus of
the lesson. The noisy disruption
caused him to stumble and fall
off his teaching stool upending
the table and all of the bubbling
glassware. When he stood back up,
he was covered head to toe in pink
bubbles, and his hair was turning a
vivid shade of lilac.

Colin had raced across the classroom before Mr Snickletinkle had hit the floor, and there was only one seat left for Trixie. She sat down quickly and quietly while the old vampire wiped himself down and recomposed himself. Trixie was dismayed to see that she had sat down to the left of Verity. Gloria was to the troll's right. Trixie knew that this would make it more complicated to talk to her about what was going on with Colin. Even more annoyingly, Colin had taken a seat at the front of the class, so she had nobody to talk to at all.

Finally, the lesson began again, and Mr Snickletinkle started to mix his potion from scratch. He explained that it was a potion to change the colour of anybody who drank it to any colour of the rainbow. This would be handy, he suggested, if they needed to camouflage themselves when out in public.

Trixie had more on her mind than potions though and spent a few minutes scribbling a note to Gloria while their teacher droned on in the background. She tried to make sure she sounded friendly but asked why she was ignoring Colin and why she was spending so much time with Verity. She passed the note to the troll who grunted and passed it on to Gloria.

While she waited for a response,

Trixie tuned back to Radio Snickletinkle and listened as he explained why it was so important to mix all of the ingredients into a boiling hot cauldron. If the ingredients were allowed to cool before the mixture was complete, the potion could end up being a most powerful poison instead. Trixie made sure to make a note of that in her book.

Trixie jumped as Verity coughed grumpily and waggled Gloria's response in front of her face.

"I am not cupid," the troll grumbled in her gravelly voice. "If you want to send love letters to people, you had better do it yourself next time. The Rocks don't do a delivery service unless it's delivery some much-needed home-truths."

Ignoring the troll's rudeness, Trixie quickly unfolded the creased paper and read Gloria's neatly written response. Apparently, she had been asked to look after Verity by Miss Brimstone. Apparently, the deputy-headmistress was hoping that the troll would give them vital information about Cromley's that could help them with the Grand High Monster's inspection.

When it came to Colin, Trixie was shocked to read that Gloria had been told by Verity that Colin had been saying mean things about her being a vegetarian, about how

It would have been amazing. Her aim was true, and the plane perfect. Unfortunately, just as Trixie was about to let go of her message, Verity gave her an evil smirk and nudged her elbow hard. Her arm flung out to the side, and the plane shot off in a completely different direction, straight towards the classroom door. The classroom door that was, just at that point, being opened by the Grand High Monster.

Time slowed right down. Trixie watched her message sail through the air like treacle. There was nothing she could do to stop it. The course was set. Her heart started to race, and she felt herself sweating as the aeroplane landed

tip-first inside the Grand High
Monster's giant ear. The classroom
went silent. Everyone had turned
to watch, including Mr Snickletinkle
who let out a small squeak as soon
as he saw where the paper had
landed.

For a second, nothing happened.
Then, like a volcano slowly

erupting and burying entire villages in its path, the Grand High Monster started to laugh. This wasn't just a small chuckle or even a medium-sized guffaw, this was a big, fat belly-laugh. And when you're as big and as fat as the Grand High Monster, there is a lot of belly and a lot of laugh. Trixie felt the tension in the room melt away and was delighted to see the sheer anger on Verity's face that her plan had failed. She breathed a sigh of relief and thought, at least I won't get into trouble for this one!

How wrong she was.

CHAPTER 5

The Torture Chamber

"I really am so very sorry! Please, can I offer you more tea?"

It was the thirty-fourth time that Miss Flopsbottom has squeaked an apology to the Grand High Monster and the twenty-fifth cup of tea that she had offered him. Trixie knew this because, for the last hour and a half, she had been sat on a very uncomfortable, very cold stone bench outside of the headmistress's office door.

She thought she'd got away with her aeroplane misdemeanour. But, as soon as Mr Snickletinkle had called for Miss Flopsbottom, despite the Grand High Monster's enormous belly laughs, Verity had made it her mission to make it clear to the headteacher that Trixie had been passing messages around in class and that was why she had tried to throw the message across the classroom. Unfortunately, as soon as Miss Flopsbottom had opened out the piece of paper, it had proved the troll's story. Now Trixie was being subjected to a performance of the very best in grovelling.

Eventually, the Grand High Monster managed to persuade Miss

Flopsbottom that twenty-five cups of tea really was his limit and that he really had better be off before some of the same tea made a reappearance on the carpet. Trixie jumped in her seat as the door swung back and the enormous man ducked into the corridor. For a second, he turned to Trixie and fixed her with a very scornful, very unhappy stare before winking enthusiastically and once again bursting into his deep, rolling laugh.

"Trixie! Please come and take a seat." Trixie tore herself away from the giant-sized man who was now wiping tears from his eyes with an old, oily handkerchief and slowly edged her way into the headmistress's office. She took a seat in front of the old wooden desk but didn't dare look Miss Flopsbottom in the eye.

"You are incredibly lucky that the Grand High Monster has seen the funny side to this little incident!" The headmistress's voice was higher and squeakier than Trixie had ever heard it before, a sure sign that she was incredibly stressed and angry. She hadn't even squeaked this much after the incident with the Halloween Parade. She sounded like somebody slowly letting the air out of a balloon. "If it were up to me," she continued, "you would be expelled permanently. This little experiment of having a normal child at Monstacademy has been nothing but trouble." Trixie's heart sank even lower than it already had been. "Luckily, the Grand High Monster has reassured me of just how important you are to this school. It shows us in a better light, he said, that we can get along with people like you.

"Instead, and there really is no stronger punishment that I can give you, I am going to sentence you to spend your lunchtimes in the torture chamber for the foreseeable future."

"Torture chamber?" Trixie yelped, sure that she'd misheard.

"Oh, don't worry!" The headmistress suddenly looked

shocked. "It's not used to torture people any more. Not for the last fifty or years or so, anyway. It used to be full of racks and iron maidens and other useful things for making children tell the truth." If Trixie didn't know better, she'd have been sure she detected a hint of longing in Miss Flopsbottom's voice. "Nowadays though, I think our caretaker Grimsby keeps the vacuum in there and maybe his mop. Anyway, you'll be spending your lunchtimes down there with Grimsby. He'll enjoy the company, I'm sure!"

The torture chamber turned out to be further underneath the castle than Trixie had ever been before. She descended seemingly endless dark flights of steps before finally stepping into a dark, echoing chamber. Green slime clung to the walls and seemed to be slowly sliding towards her as she stood watching. Moths fluttered around the single candle that had been rammed into a crack in the wall.

"Don't worry, miss. It's not that bad once you get used to it!" The lisping voice came from behind her, but when Trixie spun around, there was nobody there. "Down here, miss," the lisp sighed as though it were used to explaining this fact.

"I'm so sorry, Grimsby. You caught me by surprise!" she apologised to the diminutive caretaker. She was sure he looked like he had a few extra stitch-lines lately. Obviously the older children were back up to their old tricks.

"You'd be surprised how often I hear that!" he chuckled as he opened the single wooden door that led away from the chamber and motioned Trixie to enter first.

When she entered the torture chamber, Trixie was taken aback. Unlike the room outside, dozens of bright candles hung from ornate chandeliers suspended from the ceiling. Expensive fabrics covered wooden boxes and made serviceable seats and tables; some were even dressed with gilded silver candelabras, pewter jugs and polished cutlery. The whole effect was only slightly ruined by the grinning skeleton that had been suspended from the wall like a cheap Halloween prop.

"It's amazing what gets thrown away by the school over the

years," Grimsby said reading her mind. "Including him!" he pointed to the skeleton with a grin of his own. "The old headmaster, Mr Biggus-Bogeyus." The lisping caretaker frowned as Trixie fought to hold in a giggle. "It's a very proud name in the Bogeymen clans of the very northernmost parts of Scotland, I'll have you know. A terrific headmaster as well. Died at the ripe old age of seven hundred and sixteen. He donated his body to the school, but of course, over time, things get thrown away."

Trixie found it sad in a way, looking around at all of the fantastic and yet well-worn things. She couldn't help but wonder just how many Monsters had drunk from the goblets or been illuminated by the chandeliers over the centuries. And to think she was the very first non-monster to step inside these halls. It felt like both an honour and a weight on her shoulders.

Grimsby led Trixie to the back of the dungeon, passing by ancient torture devices that sat rusted and covered in cobwebs. At one time or another, they clearly took discipline much more seriously at Monstacademy. Pushed up against the back wall was a rotting wooden desk that looked out of place amongst all the other shiny things. On it lay a scrap of paper and an old-fashioned quill and ink.

"You're to write a letter of apology to the Grand High Monster," Grimsby said. He lurched over to a desk far taller than him that was covered in bubbling and smoking glass beakers. A loud scrape echoed off the stone walls as the caretaker dragged a stool across the flagstones before clambering nimbly up to the table where he began to pour liquids from one beaker to another.

Trixie bent her head to her work but was startled when she heard muffled voices. They'd passed too quickly to make out what was said, and she couldn't work out where they had come from.

"Grimsby? Whereabouts are we

in the school?" she asked.

"At the very bottom of the bell tower on the far side of the castle. We're a hundred metres below the main hall and deep under the hill. Why do you ask?"

"Oh, no reason." Trixie didn't want to seem weird or insane. Hearing voices wasn't a good thing even amongst Monsters.

Whatever it was, it appeared to have stopped and so, reluctantly, Trixie picked up the quill and started to write.

Dear your Grand High Monsterness...

There it was again. A small,

tinny whisper. This time the voices came through loud and clear and, suddenly, Trixie knew where they were coming from. The walls were talking.

CHAPTER 6

Voices in the Wall

Once she knew what she was looking for, Trixie quickly found the source of the voices. At the base of the dungeon walls, metal gratings connected drains and air ducts all around the castle. From a few of them, she could hear the noisy sounds of the main hall in full lunchtime mode. In others, she could make out the sounds of teachers arguing amongst themselves or moaning about students, thinking they were alone in their classrooms. The grate she wanted was at the foot of the far wall.

There, a metal grating covered a hole cut out of the brickwork. A slow trickle of water oozed through the grill and dripped into a stone gutter cut into the flagstones. It flowed slowly towards a drain where it disappeared into the darkness. The flow of the water was slowed even more by a thick green slime that coated the stone.

Trixie knelt down on the cold floor and pressed her ear as close to the grating as she dared. The water didn't look very clean, and the last thing she wanted was an ear infection. Now that she was so close, she could make out the conversation clearly. There were two voices, one of which sounded very old and out of breath. The other, however, Trixie recognised in a heartbeat.

"She's locked down in the dungeons somewhere at the minute. I don't think she'll be a problem." Trixie shuddered as the gravelly voice of Verity sounded even more malicious at the end of a drainpipe. Trixie knew that they were discussing her, and that made her feel even more vulnerable.

"And the other one? The vampire?" wheezed the second voice.

"She won't be a problem, either.

She does whatever I tell her to. She's so desperate to be popular it's depressing. Even the other girls in the group follow me like sheep. It's no wonder this place is going downhill when the Monsters can't even think for themselves. You don't need to worry."

"What about the plan? How is that coming along? Will you be ready? This is our only chance."

"It will be ready. I have everything that I need. I stole the last of the bottled badger burp this morning. It's all hidden safely away in my trunk in my bedroom. Nobody dares to mess with that. I am a troll after all!"

"How are you settling in? Do you

have everything you need?" The voice suddenly sounded concerned. "Your mother worries terribly about you, you know. We're both very proud of what you're doing, but I do hope you won't have to live amongst those horrendous excuses for Monsters for long. The moment they allowed a freak like her into the school is the moment they sealed their fate if you ask me."

"I'm fine, Dad, honestly. And Trixie's not so bad. Sad and pathetic, of course, and not very clever but very, very useful for us! When all of this is over, not only will Monstacademy be closed forever, but she will get the blame!"

"What do you have planned?" Now that Trixie knew that the second voice was Verity's dad she could hear the similarities: the same condescending tone and deep, gravelly rumble like an avalanche sliding down a mountain. She pressed her ear even closer to the grate. She could feel the stagnant water dripping down her neck but paid it no attention.

"I'm not going to tell you here. I don't know who might be listening. It will all be over by tomorrow night, and then I can come home, and Cromley's will be the only school for Monsters around here."

"And the Grand High Monster?"

The question was left hanging in the air by the older troll.

"He'll be there. Everything is taken care of."

"Promise me you'll be careful." There was the sound of two pieces of rock scraping over each other.

"Eew, Dad! Don't kiss me at school! People might be watching!"

"On the top of the Bell Tower? I doubt it, darling! Anyway, I better be off. I promised your mother I'd let her know how you were as soon as I could."

Trixie pulled herself away from the grating as the two trolls said their goodbyes. So, Verity really was planning something, and whatever it was, Gloria was in it up to her eyeballs as well. Despite being incredibly mad at her friend, Trixie knew that she couldn't let Gloria get herself dragged into whatever it was that Verity was planning.

As it was still lunchtime, Trixie knew that Gloria would be sat in the hall eating her food, but she had to find a way to escape and tell her what was going on. If Verity was telling the truth, then something big was going to happen the following night.

"Grimsby, is there a toilet down here?" she asked, trying to find any excuse to leave.

"Sorry, no." He waved her request away dismissively. He had an enormous pair of tweezers in his hands and was trying hard to pluck something wiggly and slippery from a jar filled with pale pink liquid. He had one eye closed, and his tongue was hanging out of the corner of his mouth. He noticed Trixie staring and said, "They're skunk tongues."

"They have eyes and legs!" Trixie cried out.

"Yes. It's something I'm experimenting with." The caretaker didn't seem to find tongues with eyeballs and legs even remotely extraordinary.

Trixie had to ask, despite the

urgency of finding Gloria. "Why?"

"You've heard the phrase, 'Your eyes are bigger than your belly'? Now we'll know for sure!"

"Once again...why?"

"Why not?" She couldn't argue with that. "There is a toilet at the top of the steps. Don't be too long!" Grimsby turned back to his task, cursing under his breath every time a tongue wiggled free of his grasp.

Shaking her head and feeling slightly queasy, Trixie made her way out of the torture chamber and back up to the top of the stairs. She knew she didn't have long before Grimsby would start to get suspicious and come looking for her, but the main hall was on the other side of the school.

Setting off at a jog, she did her best to duck in and out of doorways whenever a teacher wandered past. Within a few minutes she was stood, slightly out of breath, inside the main hall.

The smell of the food made her realise how hungry she was, but she knew she didn't have time for that. Instead, she weaved her way through the bustling hordes of children and finally found Gloria scraping the remains of her salad into the waste food bin. Luckily, Verity was nowhere to be seen.

Gloria dropped her plate onto

the cart and embraced Trixie as soon as she saw her. Trixie was in no mood to hug her back and tried her best to peel her friend off of her.

"I'm so sorry for what Verity did to you, Trixie. She's sorry too, you know. She wanted to tell you herself. She'll be so mad that she missed you," Gloria spluttered, eager to get her apology off her chest.

"I doubt that." Trixie knew she didn't have time to go over what happened in the classroom and decided to get straight to the point. "Listen, Gloria. Verity is bad news. I've just overheard her speaking to her dad about some big plan to get Monstacademy closed. I'm telling you, she's not here by accident. She's up to something bad—"

"Not you as well?" Gloria interrupted Trixie with a scowl. "It was bad enough that Colin thought she was trouble, but you as well?"

"Gloria, I heard her telling her—"

"Yes, her dad, you said." Gloria was so angry now. Trixie expected to see smoke shooting out of her ears. "Well, I happen to know that her dad is currently working away visiting family in the Himalayan mountains. That's where her family are from originally."

"How do you know that?"

ixie wasn't so

d she misheard? Had

ily gone mad in the

e chamber and made it all up?

"She told me!" Gloria screamed and stormed off out of the hall.

Trixie sighed and absent-mindedly grabbed a chip from the plate of a passing first-year. He turned to look at Trixie but ran away as soon as he saw the look in the eyes. Somehow, she suspected that she was going to have to do this without Gloria's help. She knew she needed Colin.

CHAPTER 7

Caught

"Can you at least hold a pencil and write it down?" Trixie was already annoyed by her brush with Gloria at lunchtime the day before, and her mood wasn't being helped by the fact that her other best friend wasn't making any sense. It wasn't his fault, though. He was currently a small, pink poodle.

Despite searching everywhere the day before, Trixie hadn't been able to find Colin anywhere and

had been forced to go to bed
unhappy and uneasy at being no
closer to solving the mystery of
what Verity was up to.

As she'd laid in bed, she'd
noticed the full moon outside her
window and known at once why
Colin was hiding away. When she'd
finally found him during a break
in classes, it was nearly lunchtime
again, and she was anxious about
how little time they had left.

To make matters worse, her only
companion was more interested in
chewing his own leg than in solving
the mystery.

"Woof."

"I don't know if that's a yes or

no! Can you at least nod or shake your head?" In all their time as friends, Trixie had never been able to get the hang of understanding Colin when he was in his other form. Gloria seemed to understand him instinctively, but then talking to and controlling animals was all part and parcel of being a vampire. Colin nodded his head. Right now, they were back in Trixie's dormitory, and she was nearly ready to throw her friend out of the window.

Trixie was also feeling very uneasy. When she'd returned to her room the night before, angry and upset that Colin was nowhere to be found, she'd discovered that one of her robes had gone missing and that somebody had emptied out all of her drawers and her wardrobe. For all she knew, other things had been taken as well. It was not like she would notice given that, in some ways, the ransacking had simply made her room tidier.

It had shaken her up considerably. She really wished that Colin was his usual, boyish self. She could do with some of his silliness right about now.

"Great. So, Verity is up to something big, and it's all planned to go down tonight. We don't have much time." She'd spent a patient half-hour telling him exactly what she had heard while in the torture chamber. She'd been slowed down considerably by the fact that Colin insisted on asking questions and that each one soundly exactly like "Woof?".

In the end, she'd managed to shut him up for long enough by handing him one of the vividly pink little treats that he so loved at this time of the month.

"The way I see it, we have one choice. Whatever she is planning, she has it hidden in her trunk. I know we've been here before," it would be a long time before Trixie forgot the smell and mess under the boy's beds when they'd gone hunting for Heston Gobswaddle's trunk the year before, "but this time you'll have to come with me.

We haven't got a third person to watch the door. It's lunchtime in ten minutes so we'll go then. Hopefully, they will be down in the hall for long enough."

Colin looked disgusted at the idea of missing a meal, and even Trixie's own stomach lodged a protest. She hadn't eaten breakfast in her rush to find Colin, something that she was now very aware of. She threw a handful of treats onto the floor and grabbed a chocolate bar from the hidden stash at the back of her chest of drawers.

"Don't tell anyone!" she ordered Colin, who she noticed had taken a sudden interest in what else might be behind there. "Let's head over there now, and we should get there just as they are heading down to eat."

Dotted around the grounds of Monstacademy were eight tall stone towers. Four of them were home to the dormitories. The others housed the classrooms and the offices of the teachers. Within each dormitory tower, there were six floors of rooms; the first-years lived on the first floor, the second-years on the second, and so on until the children reached the age of sixteen. After that, they headed off either to get a job or to one of the prestigious Atropa League Universities, the best places for a Monster to continue his or her scary education.

Since they had become best friends the year before, Gloria shared a dormitory with Trixie, but since she'd befriended the troll, Gloria was spending most of her time in the Bell Tower which, as well as the torture chamber, was home to Verity's dormitory. Trixie headed there with Colin safely stowed away in a rucksack slung over her shoulders. Every now and again, he would kick her in the small of her back if she jolted him too much or, more likely, whenever he felt like it.

It didn't take them long to pass through the rapidly emptying corridors and climb the short steps to the second floor of the tower. Trixie breathed a huge sigh of relief when she edged around the door and found the room empty. She quickly unzipped the bag and Colin tumbled out onto the floor, nipping at her ankle as punishment for what he clearly felt was a rough journey.

"Stop it!" she scolded him. "We've no time for that. Find Verity's trunk and let's get out of here."

This time it didn't take Trixie long to find the trunk she was looking for, and Colin was a little bit disappointed to be called back from finishing off a delicious if days old, half-eaten sandwich he'd found under one of the beds.

"There's a padlock on it with a code. We'll never guess the number." Trixie wedged her feet against the trunk and pulled hard on the lock. It didn't budge.

"The code is zero-five-zero-eight, though it won't do you much good back in the torture chamber!" Trixie froze. The room had been empty when they'd come in, she'd checked. But then she realised that there are oh so many places to hide in a messy dormitory.

"Verity, I—" she began as she stood to face the troll.

"Trixie! How could you?" Gloria was stood sobbing next to her new best friend. "I told you earlier that you were wrong. I'm so sorry, Verity." The fact that she was apologising to the troll made Trixie's blood boil.

"Don't apologise to her!" she screamed at the vampire. "She's the one who's up to no good, and you're going to get taken down with her because you are being so...so...stupid!" It wasn't best insult she'd ever hurled, but it was the best she could think of.

A loud bark from Colin caused them all to stop their screaming and turn around. Somehow he'd managed to enter the code into the lock, and Verity's trunk stood wide open. Inside were a dozen empty glass jars. Only a green smear on the lids hinted that they'd ever contained anything.

"See!" Gloria shouted triumphantly. "There's nothing wrong with keeping glass jars in your trunk. Though it is a little weird, Verity." This last bit was whispered out of the corner of her mouth.

"I keep a special moisturiser in them. Us trolls have to moisturise every day; otherwise, we suffer from terrible Craggies. You should see the cliffs forming on my Aunt Marbell. I've run out though, so my dad has had to race home from a trip abroad to bring me some more." Now the troll turned on the waterworks. "I hope that you're happy. I'm so embarrassed!" she wailed.

Trixie didn't believe her for a minute. After all, she'd heard the conversation at the top of the Bell Tower. She was about to say as much when Miss Brimstone stuck her head through the door and asked just what the screaming and shouting was all about.

Verity took great delight in explaining just what had happened, embellishing here or there, and it wasn't long before she was demanding the harshest of punishment for Trixie. Worryingly, Miss Brimstone just looked carefully from Trixie to the trunk and back to Verity. A quiet and calm Miss Brimstone was unnerving.

"I think you ought to speak to the Grand High Monster, Miss Grimble. Come with me."

Just as she was about to go through the door back into the corridor, Trixie turned to look at Gloria. To her utter surprise, the vampire gave her a big wink and a smile.

CHAPTER 8

An Unmonstrous Monster

"Trixie, I think it's time that you and I had a little talk." The Grand High Monster had met Trixie and Miss Brimstone at the entrance to the Bell Tower as they had descended from Verity's dormitory. Miss Brimstone had explained to the giant of a man what had happened and Trixie's part in it all. All the way through, he had simply nodded along and smiled. When he smiled, his big, bushy beard rippled like the ocean, and his caterpillar eyebrows wiggled across his forehead. Trixie couldn't help but smile back.

Miss Brimstone had muttered something about having too much work to do to sort out more problems and had left them alone in the courtyard. The Grand High Monster had led Trixie out through the back gate that led down onto the sports field and towards the large pond that had been the scene of Trixie's first Snaffleball disaster.

Every time that Trixie tried to speak, the Grand High Monster would hold his finger to his lips, so she remained silent until they were stood by the side of the pond and staring at their reflections in

the still water. This early in the
term it wasn't frozen over yet,
but it certainly looked cold and

unwelcoming.

Just as Trixie was plucking up the courage to ask what this was all about, the Grand High Monster spoke in his slow, rumbling tone. "I understand that you are having some problems with Miss Dogsby. That you think she is a spy for Cromley's." He didn't mock her when he spoke. Instead, he seemed curious to hear what she thought, and so Trixie told him everything that had happened and what she thought it meant.

"Indeed." Again, he stopped speaking and just stood in silence, seemingly lost in his own reflection. When he finally spoke, it made Trixie jump, and she very nearly slid forwards into the dark water. "Would it surprise you to know, Miss Grimble that, despite what you have been told, you are not, in fact, the first ordinary person to attend Monroe's Academy?"

It certainly did surprise Trixie, and she told the Grand High Monster as much.

"There was once a child," he continued, all the while staring deep into the water, "maybe, oh I don't know, fifty or sixty years ago, who was sent to the scary school for Monsters that sat high on the top of a hill. The story goes that when he was an infant, his mother dropped him into a

pile of horse manure and, even
though they cleaned him up well,
something of the goodness in all
that manure seeped into his bones,
and he just grew and grew and
grew until, eventually, he was
taller than the rooms in the house.

"His parents were loving and
kind and did everything that they
could to help him. They knocked
through the ceilings and added
extra rooms to the side of the
house. They took him to see
every doctor in England and every
specialist in Europe, but none
of them was able to help. In the
end, he grew too tall to attend
the lovely school to which he had
grown accustomed. He grew tired
of sitting outside and watching

lessons through the window, and his teachers grew tired of him squashing the chairs whenever he tried to sit down. I'm sure you can imagine how unhappy this made him?"

Trixie nodded her head. "It sounds horrible, that poor boy."

"Indeed. Anyway, it was at this point that his mother turned to his father over dinner one night and asked the question that would change his life. 'There is a school,' she said as he tucked into her cabbage and beetroot quiche, 'where children who are different are welcomed with open arms and given a fair chance to succeed.' His father was impressed and muttered as much.

"Of course, they were talking about Monroe's Academy, and it was decided very quickly that he should start classes here as soon as possible. He fit in perfectly. Of course, he did. He was ten feet tall with a big, booming voice. Who couldn't see that he was a monster, indeed? A Giant, they called him. But all that time he hid a great big secret. There was nothing monstrous about him at all. He was a perfectly ordinary little boy. Only he wasn't so little.

"He never told a soul his little secret. He was too worried about what the other children might think. It seems to me, Trixie, that you have your own secret to keep. You may not be a monster, but I think it is clear to us all that you are anything but ordinary. In fact, wherever you go, extraordinary things seem to happen with remarkable regularity!"

Trixie blushed at the compliment and thanked the Grand High Monster.

"Please, call me Reginald. You can leave the Trompington, though. I've had more than enough trouble for that name! As for what you have told me about Miss Dogsby, I fear that you may be correct. A dozen bottles of badger burp went missing from the store cupboard the other day, I wonder why? It's a terribly difficult ingredient that, in the wrong hands, does nothing but terrible things to any potion to which it is added. You of all people know this!"

Trixie thought back to the runaway potion that seemed so long ago now and blushed an even deeper shade of red.

"Unfortunately, without evidence, there is nothing that Miss Flopsbottom or I can do to intervene. I think that it may once again fall to the Extraordinary Trixie Grimble to save the day!" One of the caterpillars danced up and down as he winked. "Do remember though that there may be another person who realises just what her new best friend is up to. Indeed, that may well be the reason that she is such a good friend."

Suddenly it seemed so obvious to Trixie. Of course, Gloria knew what Verity was up to: she was far smarter than Trixie and Colin combined. And no wonder she was annoyed at Trixie, Gloria knew that she might ruin it all by poking around. She knew that she had to tell Colin the news and then she had to find Gloria to solve the rest of this puzzle together.

"You never asked me the boy's name?" The Grand High Monster seemed curious.

"I'm sure I know it, sir. It was you, wasn't it? You're not a Monster, either?"

The Grand High Monster winked once more and smiled.

"I am, in fact, really rather ordinary myself! Though I don't think it would be a good idea if my secret were to get out just now."

Trixie heard the little warning sound in her new friend's voice and knew that she had no choice but to keep his secret. Who would believe her anyway?

"Come. We must make a move, after all the Grand Feast in my honour is due to start soon. I'd hate to be late for my own celebration!"

The odd couple laughed and chatted all the way back to the castle. As Trixie listened to what Monstacademy had been like back when the Grand High Monster was a boy, she worked out just what she needed to do next.

CHAPTER 9

The Grand Plan

It was almost dark by the time
Trixie found Colin, and the other
children were starting to make
their way slowly towards the
main hall for the Grand Feast.
In the end, she found him curled
up asleep underneath her bed.
He'd managed to run away while
they were concentrating on Miss
Brimstone and Trixie.

When she finally managed to
wake him up by prodding him with

a long stick (which recently had played a starring role in a game of fetch), he just looked sheepish, which is quite an impressive look on a poodle.

After explaining to him everything that the Grand High Monster had told her about Verity and Gloria (she didn't even dare tell Colin about his secret identity), she urged her furry friend to his feet and ran off to find their other friend.

Once again, they found themselves running along empty corridors, but no matter how hard they searched they couldn't find Gloria anywhere. They tried Trixie and Gloria's dormitory and even raced up the stairs of the Bell Tower to find Verity's dormitory empty and dark. They tried all of the classrooms that they could think of and even found the offices of Miss Flopsbottom and Miss Brimstone empty.

It didn't take long before they found themselves outside the great doors that led into the main hall. Despite the thick wood, they could hear the sounds of the Grand Feast getting underway. It sounded like Miss Flopsbottom was giving a speech to great applause, and they knew it wouldn't be long before the food was trundled out on great silver platters and the feast itself would begin.

Trixie had no idea when Verity was planning to strike, but while the rest of the school were busy filling their faces seemed like a perfect time. She edged over to the door and eased it open a crack. Sure enough, the headteacher was stood up and was telling the gathered students just how amazing it was to have the Grand High Monster staying with them and what a wonderful opportunity it was to show him just how fantastic the children of Monroe's Academy for the Different were.

There was something odd, though. Considering this was supposed to be such an important event, Miss Flopsbottom and the seated Grand High Monster were

the only teachers in the hall.
There was no Miss Brimstone or Mr
Snickletinkle. No Grimsby. There
were no other members of staff at
all. Something was definitely going
on, and it made Trixie very uneasy.

Nobody present at the feast
noticed the big wooden door close
slowly, and Trixie raced away
unnoticed with Colin tight at her
heels. It was no use. No matter
where they looked or how quickly
they ran, they just couldn't find
Gloria.

They were soon out of breath
and out of ideas, and Trixie
slumped back against the stone
wall of a corridor somewhere near
the base of the Bell Tower.

Think, Trixie! she commanded herself. She knew she was missing something, something important. She could feel it tickling the back of her brain. If only she could join the dots. Something that somebody had told her was nagging her for attention.

Bottled badger burp.

The Grand High Monster had told her how several bottles had been stolen the other day, and Verity had even mentioned it herself. Trixie knew just what that could do to a potion. How much damage would her potion have caused if it had been let loose in an area as big as the main hall? She shuddered as she remembered how it had seemed almost alive and had spread quickly across the floor, sticking to everything and everyone that it touched.

Trixie held her breath. She could sense she was close to it now. It was like a jigsaw puzzle. She had all the pieces, she just needed to put them together. She knew that Verity wanted the Grand High Monster to close Monstacademy and the best way to do that was to embarrass the school. What better way to do that than to have them all stuck to their seats during the Grand Feast?

She allowed herself to breathe slowly. Okay, so she knew what she had planned, but how? There was no way that Verity could throw a bottle of the potion into the hall without being noticed, and she was convinced that it would all be blamed on Trixie. There had to be another way. Trixie looked down and saw that Colin had once again curled up and fallen to sleep. She couldn't be mad at him. She knew that part of being a dog meant that he just wanted to sleep all of the time, especially after such a long walk.

Then, like a lightning bolt, Trixie realised what Verity had planned. She thought back to how she had first heard about the troll's plans. The air vents connected the entire castle. She'd even heard the noise of the main hall when she was listening in to the different gratings in the wall. All she would have to do is release the potion into the correct vent, and it would spread out and do the rest.

Halfway during the feast, it would rain down from the vents in the hall ceiling, and everyone would be stuck. If Trixie hadn't been in such a panic, she would have conceded that it was, in fact, a rather brilliant plan. The only thing she wasn't sure of was how Verity was planning to blame Trixie, but for now, she knew where she needed to be.

With any luck, she'd find Gloria and the rest of the teachers on the way.

CHAPTER 10

Caught in the Act

Trixie nearly jumped right out of her skin as she raced around the last bend in the steep steps that led down to the torture chamber and came face to face with an angry vampire.

"Gloria!" Trixie wailed before being shushed into silence by her friend. Miss Brimstone and Grimsby stepped out of the shadows, and Grimsby at least smiled in Trixie's direction. Miss Brimstone continue to look as though she were sucking a lemon.

"Miss Grimble," the deputy headmistress scowled, "please do us all a favour and remain quiet. You have obviously figured out why we are all here, but your silence is appreciated. For now, we wish Miss Dogsby to remain oblivious to our presence. Miss Flopsbottom is doing a grand job of extending her speech long past the point of good taste. In a moment, Mr Grimsby and I will enter the torture chamber and put a stop to this charade. You three," she waved her hand delicately as though trying to shake off something nasty, "will remain out here."

Grimsby reached into the shadows and produced a wooden stick wrapped in cloth. A thick match hissed into flame when he struck it against the cold stone, and the torch flickered into life, casting a warm yellow light and making the shadows seem suddenly darker.

"She has snuffed out the chandeliers." Grimsby seemed more annoyed at this fact than anything else that the troll might have done.

Miss Brimstone edged over to the door, but before she could turn the handle, Grimsby darted in front of her and held up his hand for silence. With a knowing if somewhat resigned look, he touched his foot to an almost imperceptibly raised area on the dusty floor. With a speed that surprised Trixie, he immediately leapt backwards and sighed heavily as a small bucket of scorpions rained down from the ceiling and scurried off into the crevices of the stone wall.

"The little Monsters will have their fun. They're always trying to get one over on me," the be-stitched man muttered as he indicated to Miss Brimstone that it was now safe for her to proceed.

Quietly, making sure the door made as little noise as possible, Miss Brimstone and the caretaker slipped into the torture chamber. Trixie pressed her ear to the wood and felt Gloria lean against her in a bid to do the same. Colin started scratching at the floor – some impulses were too hard to fight.

From inside, Trixie heard a sharp squeak of surprise from the troll at just the same time that the door swung open on its well-oiled hinges. The two girls tumbled into the room and Colin bounded in, pushing his feet into their ears, eyes and mouths in his eagerness to be first. Trixie looked up in time to see Miss Brimstone sigh and shake her head.

By the light of Grimsby's torch, they could make out Verity

perched on top of a wooden barrel. A metal tap had been plugged into the side, and thick hose ran into the air vent. So far, nothing was flowing through it. It should be impossible for somebody made of stone to blush, but Verity was managing it very well. She started to protest, but Miss Brimstone cut her off before she could even say a word.

"Young lady, there is no point you trying to lie your way out of this one. We all know why you are down here. I must admit, if it weren't for Gloria you might very well have gotten away with it. As it happens, she realised long ago that you were up to no good. In fact, she was so determined to

bring your plan to an end that she
pushed away her best friends."
Miss Brimstone looked across
to Trixie and Colin, who were
both working on their own, very
impressive blushes. Gloria was
staring at the floor.

"Actually," the vampire

muttered, "it wasn't until Trixie and Colin found the empty glass jars in Verity's trunk that I finally understood what she was planning to do. Without their help, I might never have realised in time. It was really all of us that stopped her, Miss Brimstone." She smiled at Trixie and Colin, although he was too busy chewing his tail to notice.

"How very honest of you, Gloria. I expect nothing less. Luckily you were able to figure it out in time and bring it to my attention. By a happy coincidence, it wasn't until tonight, and so we were able to catch you in the act. How very fortunate for us!"

"It wasn't my idea!" Verity was

sobbing genuine tears. Trixie almost felt sorry for her, but then something caught her eye. Draped over another barrel of the potion was Trixie's missing robe. Her hairbrush and pencil case were scattered over the floor with the label bearing her name carefully positioned so that anybody walking into the room would see it.

"You were going to frame me!" she squealed a lot louder than she'd intended. "That's how you were so sure that I would be the one blamed for all this. That's why you told your dad that you knew people would think this potion was me again, just like last time. Was that you as well?"

"I'm afraid that was all you, Miss Grimble," said Miss Brimstone with a resigned air. Trixie blushed at the memory.

"What's this about her dad?" asked Gloria curiously.

Trixie explained about the meeting that she had heard while in detention in the torture chamber. Miss Brimstone seemed very interested to hear the details and allowed Trixie to finish her story before speaking her mind.

"We always knew that she wasn't working alone, this makes perfect sense." Miss Brimstone looked even more cold-hearted than ever. "Your father is headmaster at Cromley's, is he not? We have sent some of the Grand High Monster's personal guards there tonight. I suspect they will want to ask him some very important questions. It is the view of the Grand High Monster that Cromley's is long overdue for a new headmaster if indeed it is to remain open."

Verity sobbed loudly. Grimsby offered her a greasy square of cloth from one of his many pockets, and she blew her nose loudly.

Miss Brimstone continued her speech. "I don't know what will happen next. You will certainly not continue your education here, and it is unlikely that you will be welcome at any other school in this country. I suspect you may have to return home to the Himalayas and spend some time with your family until the name Dogsby doesn't leave such a foul taste in the mouth.

"As for the rest of us? It sounds like Miss Flopsbottom is finally rattling to the end of her little speech. I do hope the children haven't fallen asleep and drowned in their soup. I can't wait to taste the chef's Spotted Dick. He's learned how to make it specially, and I hear it's such a fine pudding!"

Several of the Grand High Monster's guards appeared at the doorway and escorted Verity and the barrel of potion out of the chamber and up into the light. Trixie and the rest followed a good distance behind and stopped to watch the troll being dragged away from the castle and into a darkened coach that what waiting at the main gates.

Then, they turned and headed towards the main hall where Miss Flopsbottom was indeed finally taking her seat to the great applause of the children. Trixie suspected the standing ovation had nothing to do with the contents of the speech and more to do with the fact that their stomachs were telling them it was long past dinnertime.

Trixie, Gloria and Colin managed
to slip in unnoticed and found
a seat at the back of the hall.
There would be time to talk about
everything that had happened soon
enough, but, for now, they wanted
to eat!

CHAPTER 11

Making Up

Once the feast was over, Gloria explained to Trixie and Colin how sorry she was for pushing them away. She'd never trusted Verity, she said, but wanted to make sure that the troll thought they were best friends so that she'd reveal even a little bit about why she had transferred.

She also confirmed Trixie's suspicions that their little book had been filled with all of the

insults they'd ever used and all
of the rumours they'd spread.
A mysterious hero had made
this known to Miss Brimstone
who had taken it upon herself
to make the Mean Ghoul's lives
very uncomfortable. There were
rumours that Grimsby might have
to clear his things out of the
torture chamber.

Verity had been very keen to
stay away from Trixie and Colin
because she was worried that they
would get into trouble whenever
Trixie messed up. Gloria said
that she had been forced by Miss
Brimstone and Miss Flopsbottom to
go along with it so that she could
find out as much information as
possible. Apparently, they thought

that another child was far more
likely to get information out of her
than any teacher.

The next day, Colin returned
to his normal self. The very first
thing he did was to find Gloria and
tell her that he forgave her. He
had been quite upset though, so
he made a point of reminding her
every now and again just to keep
her on her toes. Trixie suspected
that the enormous bone Gloria
had stolen from the kitchens may
have had something to do with him
forgiving her so quickly.

Word soon started to spread
around the castle that Verity and
her family had been deported from
England by the Grand High Monster

and forced to return to their family in the Himalayan Mountains. Over the next few terms, Verity sent occasional letters addressed to the three of them. Even though they made a point of never writing back, it was always interesting to hear about life on a different continent and at the top of a mountain.

In each letter, Verity repeatedly apologised for what she had done and told them stories of how cold it was back in the mountains and how high the snow was piled up. They learnt that it was so cold even the yaks were thinking of going on holiday somewhere warmer. In better news, though, the Yeti had decided to come out

of hiding and were now making
an effort to spend their time
doing more productive things than
scaring lonely mountain climbers.
There was even a young Yeti-ette
enrolled to start at Monstacademy
in the new year.

The letters didn't stop there.
Trixie soon started to receive
regular updates from the Grand
High Monster. He seemed to enjoy
having somebody else who was
ordinary to talk to. It took him a
long time, but finally, with Trixie's
encouragement, he admitted to
the rest of the Monster world his
enormous secret.

Other than a few old Monsters
who were stuck in their ways (and

who doesn't know somebody like
that), nobody was very much
bothered, deciding that, all in
all, he was doing a jolly good job
and could keep on doing it as far
as they were concerned. Luckily,
nobody listens to old Monsters
anyway.

Much to Trixie's surprise,
Christmas came and went, and
spring soon turned into summer
with a complete lack of further
adventure. She was glad of it,
she told herself. It meant that
she could concentrate on her
schoolwork, and she started to
make good progress, even winning
a love-potion competition that
Mr Snickletinkle held one hot
summer's day.

It was a little bit boring, though. A little too...ordinary, she thought. She decided she'd have to do something about it soon. She couldn't go through the rest of her life with nothing exciting happening.

And then it happened. On the last day of the summer term, right when the long summer holidays were stretching out in front of them, Colin came racing into the girls' common room. His face was red with excitement, his hands were shaking, and he could barely speak a word without stuttering.

"We've been selected!" he finally managed to splutter. "I was bored the other day and signed us up for

Miss Brimstone's summer camp. We're going to study ancient monsters on the other side of the world!"

"You did what?" Gloria threw herself to her feet. "Why didn't you tell us?"

"Dunno really." Colin looked sheepish. "I just put our names down then forgot about it."

Trixie didn't say anything. This was more like it. An adventure on the other side of the world sounded like just the thing to break the boredom of a summer holiday.

"You need to pack quickly. We leave tomorrow!" Colin pulled his already packed suitcase into the room. Socks and pants stuck out of the side like tongues. "We're heading to Peru."

"Peru? What is there in Peru?" Gloria asked.

"We're going to study the ancient vampires of Machu Picchu! I thought it would be right up your alley. Apparently, some of them were vegetarian as well."

Now, even Gloria was excited. The girls quickly grabbed up their things and followed Colin through the door and off on what would no doubt be another exciting adventure.

Make Your Own Slimy Potion

If you want to make your own slimy potion, follow these simple instructions. Remember to keep a bottle of *Ranae Defricatus Urina* handy!

You will need:

100ml PVA glue
½ tsp bicarbonate of soda
Food colouring (the gel type works best)
1 tsp contact lens solution
Glitter!

What to do:

Mix the bicarbonate of soda with the glue in a large bowl.
Add drops of food colouring until your potion turns the perfect colour.
Stir in the contact lens solution and knead until it becomes slimy. You can add the glitter now if you like!

Remember, don't let Miss Brimstone catch you!

Spot The Difference

Can you spot the ten differences in these pictures?

About The Author

Matt Beighton is a full-time writer, born somewhere in the Midlands in England during the heady days of the 1980s. He is happily married with two young daughters who keep him very busy and suffer through the endless early drafts of his stories.

Matt's books have been read around the world and awarded the LoveReading4Kids "Indie Books We Love" and Readers' Favorite 5 Star Awards.

Having spent many years as a primary-school teacher, Matt Beighton knows how to bring stories to life. He regularly visits schools and runs creative workshops that ignite a passion for words.

If you have enjoyed reading this book, please leave a review online. Your kind words really do keep authors going!

To find out more visit
www.mattbeighton.co.uk